Our little Star

A book of original poems for your enjoyment and to raise precious funds for Young Lives vs. Cancer

LINDA KNIGHT

Cover image by: Linda & Tony Knight
Book design by: Taylor Knight Books

Printed in the United Kingdom First Printing, 2023

ISBN: 978-1-7394864-2-6 (Paperback)

ISBN: 978-1-7394864-3-3 (eBook)

Taylor Knight Books
19 Peters Close

Locks Heath, Southampton SO31 6EH, UK

FOREWORD - CHILDHOOD CANCER

Every year, there is a childhood cancer awareness month but raising funds for Young Lives Vs Cancer is vital all year round.

In 2020, our youngest grandson Louis was diagnosed with an aggressive form of cancer, Burkitt Lymphoma, at just 2 years old.

It was heartbreaking for the whole family but particularly for his sister and parents, who went through and continue to experience extremely anxious times.

See an article relating to Louis at the time:-

https://www.theargus.co.uk/news/189 53855.louis-knight-worthing-receives-bravery-award-cancer-research-uk/

This children's poetry book is dedicated to Louis, his sister Isabelle, our son and daughter in law, Chris and Nicki who like so many other families, have been extremely brave despite their lives having been changed forever.

As grandparents we, like so many other family members, feel the pain that our children and grandchildren, are suffering especially during the time spent waiting for the results of Louis' six-monthly check-ups.

Every single day spent with our children and our grandchildren is precious to us.

ANCESTRAL ROOTS

Our family history takes us on many searches

With research in Record Offices and various churches

We've been doing this for many years

But it's been well worth it, despite some tears

Taking photographs, meeting some new cousins

Just a few newfound relatives but not dozens

Learning your family history is to know yourself

After all, we can't pick our family off a shelf

It's very important to find names and places

Then through photographs, you also have faces

What jobs they did, where did they go
to school

Our ancestors are forgotten as a
general rule

Let's not forget them, bring them to life

Where there's children, there's a
husband and wife

Over each new discovery, we always
rave

It's so exciting when we find a new
grave

ANTS

Ants are scavengers for sweet things like melon

But they also bit the bottom of Auntie Helen

We had the sweet melon whilst we were out together

It was a lovely day with some nice warm weather

It was part of our picnic day that we had as a family

But the ants joined in and made it a double whammy

Ants come in colonies and so outnumbered us too

When it came to eating lunch, we were in a long queue

After returning back home we'd been taken over by ants

we all had bites on our bottoms and ants in our pants

BEDTIME

I know that you're feeling extremely tired

A yawn escaped your mouth as it transpired

I can clearly see you don't want to give in

But you need your beauty sleep so let's begin.

You may want to stay downstairs and by the TV sit

But you need lots of sleep time, so as to stay fit

We can't do what we want to, you must know

Grown-ups have lots of knowledge and so

If you don't want to feel sleepy at school

Settle down in your bed so don't be a mule

You need to go up now to your comfortable bed

So, you can put down and rest your weary head

On your pillow is where your head needs to be

So, you're up in the clouds, snoring loudly you see

It won't take long to begin dropping off to sleep

Upstairs you go, let's not hear another peep

Try staying asleep until at least seven o'clock

Or you'll be tired and in a complete shock

Otherwise, you'll be overtired and really sorry

It'll be hard to concentrate and then you'll worry

You might drop off to sleep whilst you're at school.

Especially as you're switched on as a general rule

Don't spoil your education when you are doing well

Empty your head don't spoil that sleeping spell

You'll be up in the morning feeling very refreshed

Climb out of your bed and get washed and dressed

Breakfast time should be something energetic to eat

Then you'll feel full of beans whilst sitting in your seat

You can look forward to another brand-new day

Before tonight when you will once more hit the hay

Don't slacken just yet as there's homework to do

Whilst listening to some music as it is relaxing too

Wind down time happens following on from dinner

A tune you enjoy, then we're onto a winner

BRANCHING OUT

I decided to climb Grandad's garden
trees

It's like being at height on a circus trapeze

I'm so high and so much closer to the sky

Now I've reached the top, I'm thinking why?

It seemed a good idea at the time to me

Now I'm stuck up here on the branch of a tree

How will I get down from my big adventure?

I need to think carefully before I even venture

I'm back down now, taking it slowly and carefully

It's embarrassing as my parents could see me

I got myself in this mess so now I need to cope

At this moment in time, I just need some hope

I've been a silly boy so I need to stop and think.

Put myself in their shoes and not even blink

I climbed the tree on a spur of the moment

At the end of the day, it was also enjoyment

I've learned from this and also come through

Looking back on this I didn't have a clue

BULLYING

It's not cool to be a person who likes to bully

To be treating someone else like a line pully

Pushing and pulling them from side to side

Respond to it but please don't let things slide

If this is happening to a friend or perhaps you

Stop this awful misery now for your sake too

Tell an adult and ensure that you are found

Don't let yourself be wrestled to the ground

Make it clear they don't need to be so tough

You're strong like the bullies but not so rough

Protect yourself but be sure to do it safely

Defend your corner but do it very carefully

It doesn't matter what the reason might be

You must tell an adult whatever you see

Learn to defend yourself in whatever you do

It's important you see but especially for you

Don't be unhappy or put up with any bully

Just walk away from them, don't be used fully

It's cruel and unkind and should never go amiss

Stand up for yourself don't put up with distress

Speak up for yourself and talk to the Head

If all else fails, try stopping the culprits instead

Walk away from what's happened to take a stand

Be happy what you've done and have achieved

You should feel very proud and also be relieved

By standing your ground, a bully backs away

So, then you should feel safe and happy to stay

Whatever you need and whatever you do

Remember to always remain happy too

CAMPING

Nannie and Grandad pitched up their tent

They're in the garden being quite content

Toasting marshmallows on a hot barbeque

Not intending to eat too many - or too few

Enjoying the fresh air, wrapped up warm

Hoping there won't be an overnight storm

An eery hooting of an owl in the distance

He continues like that as he has persistence

The moon continues to light up the dark skies

The owl stops hooting so he takes off and flies

Nannie and Grandad settle down for the night

Before they're awoken and receive such a fright

They've been joined in the tent by a large fluffy cat

Who's digging its claws into the groundsheet mat

He sees a bird through the tent and runs at speed

Chasing it fast with prowess, as he feels the need

To show off his many skills and also ability

But fails to catch the bird despite his agility

Nannie and Grandad go back to sleep

And until the morning, they don't hear a peep

CASTLE

A castle can seem like a fort for a young boy

To me, I have it as an imaginative toy

Wearing a coat of armour with a fake sword

Something for battle that you might afford

A castle for a princess dressed prettily in pink

Being rescued from a tower and creating a stink

Waiting for a prince to help her become free

When he'd rather be climbing an old apple tree

Next to the castle is a moat with some water in

Waiting for a great adventure to begin

From the fortress of the castle, it's quite a sight

Careful now, it's really quite a dizzy height

The Union Jack flag flaps well in the breeze

From the tower overlooking the stormy seas

Let's go and explore the ruins, you young rascal

Go careful climbing the old stairs of the castle

Hold on really tightly to the thick wooden rope

A long and windy staircase with quite a steep slope

When you reach the top, be sure to wait for me

It's very high up and you need to stay close, you see

CATS

Cats come in many types and breeds

They can run fast and at various speeds

Hairless cats are bald and quite wrinkled

Other cats have fur that's well sprinkled

Different shades of colour and fur length

Cats don't recognise their own strength

Some are elegant, sleek and content

They like to ensure their day is well spent

By chasing birds with claws on their prey

It's a natural instinct for a cat to play

They then rest and sleep the rest of the day

Where they can curl in a ball inside of a bed

So, they rest themselves on their weary head

They like to bask quietly away from the sun

Then awaken, stretch out, frolic and run

Chase butterflies and birds playing along

Waiting at the bottom of a tall garden tree

In the hope of taking a bird home for tea

If successful they will carry it back home

Through the cat flap where humans will groan

The cat is shocked as the bird is still alive

As it wriggles and jiggles to try and survive

His mum she checks out the lively small bird

Then tuts at the cat and has a sharp word

The cat watches on as the bird is released

Then mutters 'I thought it was deceased'

But now she'll settle down as it's dark

The cat has decided to be up with the lark

CEREAL KILLER

Why add nasties to our breakfast cereal

When additives can be very immaterial

Sugar and colours can make them tasty

Remember though don't be so hasty

Colours might look nice on the surface

Don't turn them into a colourful circus

Making them crunchy and appealing

Remember that parents also have feelings

When dealing with food colour reactions

Don't sit back and say it just happens!

Invent something that is nice to eat

But no sugar and colours to complete

Add natural flavours that can appeal

It can make breakfast much more ideal

By all means add some flavour and spice

To make them tasty and especially nice

Children like food that's good for you

So, make their dreams and wishes come true

CHRISTMAS EVE

It's Christmas Eve now, dear girls and boys

Time to get into bed, there'll be plenty of toys

Santa will be doing his toy rounds all night

Hang up your stockings as the time is right

Close your eyes, go straight off to sleep

That's good girls and boys, shhh not a peep

Leave Santa some beer and a nice mince pie

He will be spying with his beady little eye

Give Mummy and Daddy their kisses goodnight

He'll see you all later when he visits you all right?

He used to climb down the chimneypot you see

But nowadays he has a special magic key

He will try his best to guess what you'd like

Did you make a list and did he see a new bike?

There's quite a good selection for him to choose

You will always win but nobody will ever lose

When all the children awake early in the morning

Parents that are woken at 5 am are still yawning

But, at the end of the day it's only once a year

So, enjoy your children's happiness and their cheer

Happy Christmas to all of you as you are very dear

<u>CHRISTMAS TIME</u>

Christmas time, it's time to get together

For family to gather around us whatever

The moon is above and shaped like a crescent

We know that you can't wait to unwrap a present

A time when the snow could possibly fall

That's something that nobody knows at all

Christmas time with family is for you and me

Baubles, tinsel, mistletoe and tree

The clock on the shelf is ticking and tocking

Better check, have you hung up your Christmas stocking?

Smelling spices, Christmas pudding and of course the cake

Especially when they are so wonderful to make

Traditional Christmas dinner, hat and some crackers

Whatever we eat, family are always what really matters

CITY

The city is so busy unlike the countryside

Full of people travelling to work in suits, with pride

People walking at a fast pace, needing plenty of space

Needing to slow down more because it's not a race

In a hurry getting to work or be on their way home

Be sightseeing at museums or the London dome

There's lots for a family to do in the city

But it can be quite expensive, which is such a pity

It's worth a trip there for a really special treat

Maybe the theatre if you book the right seat

CONFIDENCE

Sometimes we pretend to be tough as well as brave

To put a tough coating on and then begin to crave

The confidence we would like in a very large heap

Stopping the sadness and sometimes lack of sleep

As we grow older, we gradually start to change

Feeling more confident and begin to engage

To communicate with friends and your family too

Remember you can do it now go show us you,

It's all about having the courage or the confidence

To do it you just need to use some common sense

CYCLES

Cycles can have 2 or 3 spoked wheels.

Not everyone can race upon their heels

To climb up onto their saddle takes
ability

It also takes a certain amount of agility

To ride a bike takes plenty of good skill

To pedal up a a mountain or even a hill

Ensure the child comes out in you well

By having a horn or a really loud bell

If someone gets far too close to you

Press the horn or bell to warn them too

A bright coat so you are seen to be there.

And a bright pair of gloves to say, beware

That way you should always be noticed

By drivers who haven't got the remotest

It's good for you to be out in the fresh air

With the wind blowing on your dark curly hair

Hoping it stays warm and also dry today

As you set off on your happy, merry way

A picnic and drink to enjoy on your break

Hoping it stays dry or it could be a mistake

I'm not prepared for any rain as you can see

But the forecast says that it's going to be

The perfect day out in the country breeze

With a cycle helmet upon my head, we've seized

Sunglasses to protect my eyes from the sun

Pedalled quite some distance and now I'm done

Time to head back home as it's time for dinner

I have finished for the day and onto a winner

CYRIL THE SQUIRREL

Cyril the squirrel's in the garden tree

He climbs down, to come and visit me

When Cyril visits, he does his very best

To stand and show off his little white vest

Running round the garden he likes eating

Playing with friends and then repeating

Over the day, Cyril and friends come to visit

They enjoy our squirrel food as a
requisite

As the light starts fading, it's time for
bed

He jumps in the tree and homeward
heads

DADDY LONG LEGS

A daddy long legs lands upon my head

His long legs tickle me and this I dread

A cranefly with strange paper like wings

A long thin body that hovers round things

June to September they're out and about

When in the house I really have no doubt

That the long-legged fly will be hiding there

In the corner of a room but not sure where

They're always silent and try not to be heard

If they go outside, they'll be eaten by a bird

Its other name is a leatherjacket

Please do not be tempted ever to whack it

They are not poisonous and can't even bite

So absolutely no reason for you to take a fright

Just watch it and wonder when it starts to hover

It could be a child looking for his father or mother

DEREK THE DUCK

Derek the duck is nervous as he quacks and quakes

 When he hears loud sounds, he applies his brakes

He cannot run too fast or he trips over his webbed feet

As they appear to make him feel like he's lifting concrete

He waddles along before losing his balance

His bottom goes in the air, just like a bed valance

He's had a lot of problems since he was a little duckling

But now he's an adult, his legs feel like they're buckling

He was never taught to swim or how to move along

So, Derek just waddled and tried to stay strong

He now can get some help from friends just like you

Then he should be able to waddle along just like he ought to

DOGS

A dog is variable in its breed and size

With a wet nose and bright shiny eyes

A glossy coat and a tail that can wag

My collar's got my name on it with its shiny tag

I don't bark except when I need to talk

Usually when I need to go out for a walk

Be nice, feed me something good please

Don't touch my coat, in case I have fleas

Don't startle me or shout really loud too

You could frighten me into a premature poo

I'm really quite nice though sometimes I drool

It doesn't happen often as a general rule

A walk by the sea is good when it is warm

I'll stay close but hide when there's a storm

Sometimes I might need a visit to the vets

For routine stuff like vaccines for woolly pets

Sometimes I get an itch and need some cream

The itch scratch cycle may seem a bit extreme

DREAMING

The dreamer looks out of the window in class

Concentrating as they stare through the glass

Their mind is not hearing or seeing very much

As it wanders elsewhere not thinking as such

What are you thinking of in your dream world

As you start to adjust and your thoughts unfurl

The teacher startled me from my deep dreams

A tap on the shoulder awoke me, it seems

Maybe write down what you're thinking, my dear

The teacher suggested and made it quite clear

She wasn't amused at the teacher's suggestion

But couldn't answer as she didn't know the question

Perhaps there was a solution to the puzzle itself

But couldn't find it as she couldn't reach the shelf

Books have answers but could this one be solved

We're sure it will but the class might be involved

How complicated is this dream for observation

Because I was dreaming and lost my concentration

DUVET DAY

I'd really like to take a duvet day

Relaxing and watching the telly hey

Having a lie-in and playing with my toys

Whatever I do it will make some noise

Turning the tv volume higher than ever

So, I can hear the words as I am clever

Spending some time in the garden too

Practising football and kicking it to you

I would not make a habit of skiving school

It wouldn't be good and could never be cool

I'm really not pulling too many strings here

I'll not be loud so you'll hardly know I'm there

EARWIGS

Earwigs have a thin shiny long brown body

With their coat of armour like a squaddie

Their sharp pincers are ready for another attack

As they lunge forward in a clumsy stack

They have grasshopper style, bent up legs

That look quite a bit like long broken pegs

Sometimes they can seem to look scary

They're certainly not ever at all hairy

They usually come out at night-time ,see

So please go careful you don't step on me

I could get squashed flat as I am nature

Remember when having a garden adventure

To look where you put your feet down first

Or this earwig could be crushed and burst

saying it's unlikely to happen in defence

As they scamper and disappear past the fence

He normally runs along quite slowly and knows

When humans are sensed, he hides and goes

On his way perhaps under a branch or two

Where you won't find him and he won't see you

EASTER

When it's Easter it can be nice and sunny

It's traditionally time for the Easter bunny

There can also be an Easter bonnet procession

To show creativity and colour like an obsession

Springtime comes with new flowers and shoots

Some April showers followed by wellington boots

Children love to take part in an Easter egg hunt

Watch your eggs as somebody might play a stunt

Christians believe Jesus may have risen again

Others choose not to go to church and refrain.

Daffodils are being picked for their yellow yields

Lambs running through daisies in the fields

Enjoy your Easter whatever you do

But please don't eat too much chocolate, you

FEELINGS

We all get cross and annoyed but don't burst

Try not to react but please stop and think first

You could regret getting verbal with each other.

Stop and wait don't get into more bother

Make the choice and stay firmly in control

Even if that person drives you up the pole

Try to be patient and don't quickly react

Remember to answer with a little more tact

We all have feelings and strong opinions too

But we also need to think a bit of others, you

Never hit or attack anyone with your bare hands

Or even think of doing something much more grand

Say sorry now, don't hesitate or even worry

Set good examples, don't rush or even hurry

Show your affection but never aggression

It's important to be giving a good impression

Shake hands or hug to show it's all over and done

Don't ask whether you have lost or even won

We are all equal and need to receive respect

Think of the consequences and the after-effects

After all they are usually someone in your family

That's a good reason not to get in a huff angrily

Say sorry but mean it and show them you care

Instead of getting cross, just give them a stare

With hands on your hips looking in a rage there

Stop! think why it's happening and say no more

Remember they're family both now and before,

You'll only be in trouble otherwise so don't do it

Be kind and hug say sorry please do not ever hit

It is just a difference of opinion after all and so

Don't even think about stamping on their toe

Agree to disagree, turn and walk away from this

No winding them up, a hug wouldn't go amiss

The argument is now over and finished right

So go up to your room and out of our sight

I'm disappointed that you thought it was okay

To attack and put your anger on public display

A little more patience is needed from you

To show that you care and didn't mean it too

FOGGY DAY

It's a very damp cold foggy morning

The sound from the foghorn sends out
a warning

Out in the Solent, they watch fore and
aft

Looking for danger that might sink their
craft

The lighthouse does it's best to light
and shine

In the murk and the gloom, sailors look
for a sign

Don't hide in the fog, well away from
me

It can be thick and patchy, so difficult to
see

Breath steams when blowing in the air

A dampness you simply cannot
compare

Fog takes time to clear through the day

But eventually much later, it will go away

FOOTBALL BRILLIANCE

Our grandsons' love to play a game of football

They enjoy the training and the game overall

The challenges and skills that go along with it

Making friends too and becoming quite a hit

It takes skill to play football and we show our feelings

Receiving a trophy from hard work is quite appealing

Scoring goals gives a huge sense of achievement

Don't argue with the ref or have a disagreement!

It is about making an effort and trying your best

At half time drink water and take a little rest

When it's cold you need to keep moving around

Don't get tripped up or you could hit the ground

Just enjoy the match that you are taking part in

Try concentrating on the game followed by the win

Remember don't get disappointed if you lose

There's always next time so long as you choose

To continue along your footballing journey

Well done boys for getting up so early

Practise makes perfect, remember that too

The more you play off pitch, the better you do

FRENCHIE

One of our dogs is Percy the Frenchie

He is muscular but   sometimes stenchy

A short broad body and black glossy coat

With wrinkled skin around nose and throat

He's loyal and enjoys being sat upon my lap

When moving around his oversized ears flap

He doesn't like being at home on his own

Or he can get rather anxious when all alone

Percy can become easily overheated you see

So needs plenty of water and being close to me

Swimming is definitely out of the question

Don't say it please, it's a really bad suggestion

I have a playmate named Frankie and he is a pug

We are both the same and we like a hug

Our family they are the best you know

Cos' they nurture us and keep us on the go

Little exercise is needed for me or Frankie

As we get tired and occasionally cranky

Frankie is more of a pensioner than me

But he nevertheless keeps me company

GRANDADS ROOTS

Grandad's a Brummy through his Birmingham roots

He walks through the countryside in his welly boots

Travelling back to The Midlands in our motorhome

There's no restriction on the distance he will roam

Back to his old Warwickshire childhood living

In a country cottage from his humble beginnings

Some roads to Maxstoke, where he lived as a child

They were really narrow and others quite wide

Looking across at the farmer's fields and furrows

Where in the distance you can see the rabbit burrows

Going way back in time to his old photographs

Where Grandad flicked cow pats for fun and a laugh

Those were the days, he says as times were carefree

In the fields playing from breakfast time up until tea

No watch to check, just loads of time to play

Or sneezing as he rolled over in the hay

At times in the city when he wasn't in a hurry

He would stop off after work for a balti curry

Memories are so precious, bottle that thought

Remembering good times just as you ought

GREENERY

Green is a lush colour that comes in many shades

It's the way that nature intended it to be made

The forest and the countryside are lush and also green

This allows for all its beauty to stand out and be seen

The heat can make the grass turn crisp dry and brown

When the sun burns on the grass that is when it's found

Green is for go, like part of a traffic light sequence.

Being amongst nature makes such a big difference

Walking through grass in a meadow full of flowers

Summertime is when the grass grows fast and towers

Countryside shows outside space utilised to its best

Where animals can roam freely and can take their rest

HAIR

Hair can be straight or naturally curly

Sometimes dishevelled when up very early

There are many different shades of colour too

Not always natural but that's entirely up to you

There are lots of ways to change a hairstyle

When it hasn't been different for a while

Hair, it grows gradually upon your head

It grows on you but it can sometimes shed

A brush and comb are style essential

For making your hair all quintessential

Long hair, short hair or in-between

Having it wavy just like the last queen

How we style our hair is individual to you

Perhaps not too drastic, remember that too

Patients with cancer can also lose their hair

Support and fundraising, helps to show we all care

So please donate to support children with cancer

Only lots more research will help find the answer

<u>HAMSTERS</u>

These elongated short balls of colourful fluff

Running at speed make you feel out of puff

Inside their wheel, they run round and round

With their little pink feet, they make little sound

Filling their cheeks up full, with lots of food

Then hiding it in their bedding where it gets stewed

Spending hours energised and running on the go

Then going back to bed and settling down slow

Their short round bodies stand on their legs

Looking as though they have the need to beg

With sawdust laying on the ground of their cage

Getting madly scuffed when they take central stage

Their thin paper like ears are very alert.

They can hear the slightest sound and then revert

The humans come down in the morning and see

The short round pom pom's cage smells of wee

A good clean of the cage is done thoroughly now

Before she awakens and scuffs sawdust somehow

HAYFEVER

My hay fever causes my nose to be blocked

I can't smell too well but I'm not really shocked

My eyes are streaming and are very itchy too

But I have eyedrops to help me to get through

Achoo, achoo, now I'm badly sneezing

My chest is so tender, I appear to be wheezing

Knowing the pollen count is extremely high

Makes me sigh and raise my eyelids to the sky

I like to smell flowers but they make me sneeze

Instead, I wear my sunglasses so enjoy the breeze

The hay fever season has been most of this year.

Not good as it calls for boos and no cheer

HOT SUN

It's really hot and your clothes get wet

As perspiration happens, or should I say sweat?

A fan on a cool setting will help for a time

An icy drink with some lemon & lime

It's so important to stay hydrated

Your liquids need to be reinstated

Drink plenty of fluids, especially water

Then you'll stay refreshed just as you oughta

Keep topping up fluids through the day and the night

Keep hydrated and stay comfortable and just right

Wear cotton and linen clothing to try and stay cool

Wear a tee shirt and shorts as a general rule

If it's summer, wear sunscreen and please take a hat

Avoid the peak heat times, don't get burnt like that

It's really not worth it to bake in the sun

Short spells outside are enough & you are done

Remember the damage it does to your skin

It's not worth the risk take this advice in

Skin cancer it really can be a killer

Remember the sun isn't always a thriller

ICY WEATHER

It's cold outside and the temperature is dropping

Hoping this unpleasant weather won't be stopping

A thin white frosty layer resting on the ground

Making it slippery like a skating rink I have found

Careful when you dare to venture anywhere outside

As you could fall on the ice and then slip and slide

Ice causes us to be cautious so we go really slow

Especially in the garden when it's going to snow

A pair of robust boots that are tough and strong

Holding onto to something carefully as we move along

A hat, a scarf, some gloves and some nice warm socks

Brr, my hands and my feet feel just like ice blocks

It's really becoming so very cold and also looks grey

Hoping that there won't be many snow flurries today

If it snows, then we'll have a lots of snowball fights

Then we can put our problems completely to rights

Taking any tension out on some wet fluffy snow

It can be quite helpful when you're on the go

If the snow begins to become much deeper

It will be time to brush it off the garden sleepers

As the snow flutters softly down to the ground

A robin in the garden tree is seen hopping around

Cat paw prints are being made in the snow

As it passed through quickly when it's on the go

When we went off to bed, the snow was still there

We awoke the next day and the ground was quite bare

The snow had melted quickly into no more than a puddle

Let's go back in the house to get warm with a cuddle

A nice hot cocoa with our hands wrapped around a mug

Staying cosy with a blanket and a nice warm rug

I'M BORED!

To say that you're bored is not totally
true

There's always something that can be
thought of to do

Whether playing a board game now
that could be fun

To playing in the garden when that is
finished and done

Something artistic and creative that
you've invented

Whatever it is please be happy and
really contented

Try to make it interesting so that others
can do

Let your friends and their mothers
have a go too

From a sport or a craft or maybe
swinging from trees

Or something that will get you onto
your knees

Whatever it is, perhaps some cooking
or baking

It will be lots of fun, that there's no
mistaking

ISLE OF WIGHT DAY TRIP

We went on a day trip to the Isle of Wight

With our buckets and spades, it was alright

We got off the ferry after it docked at Cowes

Took the bus up the hill, past Queen Victoria's house

Islanders call Newport their capital city

It's really a town which is such a pity

We took the double decker bus and went to Ryde

For a walk on the sand until the incoming tide

With suncream on and our sunhats on our head

Stayed on the beach with sunglasses until it's time for bed

A day where we made the most of our time together

Before the day changed and we had some bad weather

JELLY

A raspberry jelly turned out of its mould

Don't knock the table or lo and behold

The jelly will bounce and go out of control

On the floor and splat, it landed on my doll

She was not impressed by the messy jelly

As it continued to wobble towards my welly

The boot needed wiping or it would get smelly

All of this from a raspberry jelly that moves

As it bounces and wobbles into all the grooves

Of a chair or a floor where it waits to be found

Hoping there will be no slip ups on the ground

Fortunately, there was another one for tomorrow

That was handy as I was then able to borrow

It in advance you see when comes tomorrow

It's unlikely there won't be any leftover jelly

But by then there will be too much inside my belly

So, by then we'll be wibbly wobbling from the inside

Where it will melt, digest and then slowly subside

JENNY WREN

My Dad used to point out Jenny Wren in a tree

But I never saw the wren as I was just three

With a vertical tail and a pair of short flappy wings

Brown and short bodied but that's one of those things

Her voice can be quite vocal amongst a crowd

As people pass, her voice can seem loud

When hopping across from a tree branch

It's quite hard work as she flaps to enhance

She can build nests from the ground to up high

But it certainly won't be built on clouds in the sky

She likes mealworms and seed mixes to eat

She's the nicest Jenny Wren that you'd ever wish to meet

KITE

A kite on a string with a long-twisted tail

It takes skill and practise to get it to sail

High up in the air, flying like a bird feeling free

Diving and swooping quite close to the sea

A good wind blowing makes for good flight

The kite flies well making a colourful sight

Children love flying their kites right up high

Soaring higher and higher in the windy sky

It's a good idea to stay well away from trees

As a kite can tangle quickly, so needs to be free

Kites sometimes tangle and may cause damage

Be careful freeing it and then you should manage

To remove the kite with ease from a high tower

Takes a lot of strength and plenty of willpower

Stay away from long grass or you could trip

As your kite is very important, so try not to slip

Up on your bottom, you could slide upon a slope

Where it's not always easy to stop or even cope

Down the slope you go into the great unknown

Where the wild wind causes you to be blown

LOUD

If you want to be loud then by all means shout

It's a stress reliever so please try getting it all out

Scream if you need to but please not too loud

Even if you prefer to think that you're allowed

You need to have plenty of enjoyment in life

Enjoy your time be happy without any strife

If you happen to get cross make a loud sound

By stamping your feet firmly on the ground

Clap your hands and then sing happily along

Do all of this to the beat of your favourite song

Add some movement and dance to all of this

It could even turn out to be a hit or even a miss

Keep on moving along to the sound of the beat

It doesn't need approving so just tap your feet

Stomp those feet, practise, move right along

Knowing you'll feel happy if you also sing strong

MOTORHOME

Grandad stepped inside their Motorhome

To go out with Nannie and off for a roam

Loaded with food and fresh Granary bread

Cram packed with a perfectly yummy spread

Nannie looked forward to their day together.

But Grandad he was concerned about the weather.

He thought it would be difficult to be fully prepared

Never mind, I'm here now as he stood and stared

As they set off on the start of their days journey

Wherever it would be, they could be a little bit early

As they arrived at a place quite close to the sea

The rain it was pouring down really heavily

Grandad turned on the Calor gas outside

The door swings back and hits his backside

"My bottom!" Grandad shouted, extremely loud

Nannie shouted "look there's a big grey cloud"

Grandad was grumpy but was trying to behave

So, Nannie smiled and gave him a wave

She knew that his pride would be quite bruised.

In addition to this, he wouldn't be amused

They stayed where they were tucked up inside

With their food and drink they were able to hide

The rain stopped and a rainbow appeared in the sky

Grandad was happy but the sun shone in his eyes

Out came the shades to protect him from the glares

Think I'll pop outside to get some fresh air

Grandad's watching the water rippling out at sea

When a freak wave soaked him just before his tea

He muttered to himself and shook himself down

He wasn't happy and thought he could have drowned

Back in the motorhome for a shower and change

Nannie said don't worry it seems a fair exchange

Here's a hot cup of tea to warm you through

That should be ok or at least it should do

Let's relax and enjoy the rest of our day

This wet weather could be here to stay

NANNIE'S COOKING

Nannie loves cooking, she does it rather well

Grandad likes to sample food that's if he can smell

The aroma from the kitchen has tempted him in

Curiosity to taste, he hopes it's not from a tin

He dare not say that his nose it's totally blocked

He'll have to take a guess that it could be from a wok

Would you like to sample it? Nannie starts to ask him

It's an experiment I made up and invented at a whim

He hadn't a clue whether it was savoury or even sweet

Until much later when it started to repeat

Grandad was hoping it might be a lamb casserole

Or maybe a cake being mixed so he could lick the bowl

NEDDY THE DONKEY

Neddy the donkey is always steady

He's always happy and usually ready

Travelling along a road in the New Forest

He honks as he sees his little friend Horace

Cautious Neddy stamps his hooves

Swishes his tail and shows off his moves

A happy fellow who has lots of friends

Stomping as he approaches the bends

He continues along on his merry old
way

Having seen his lady friend Freda today

He takes a rest under an old ancient
tree

It's raining so he shelters to stay dry,
see

When it's stopped raining, he can move
on

Where once more he may come upon

Another friend whom he seems to
know

When he was young, he knew this girl
Flo

Neddy rests up as he's had a very long
day

Where in some deep woods he hides
safely away

OUR LITTLE STAR

Our grandson Louis stands out a very
long mile

From all the stars shining through with
a huge smile

His braveness and humour when aged
merely two

May in addition have helped him to get
through

Throughout the tough treatment for his cancer

This small boy has fought through with his banter

It's been a while now since he rang the chemo bell

Because regular check-ups help him to stay well

Three years have passed since he was first diagnosed

But so far, he continues to stay fully composed

It's lovely seeing Louis and his big sister Isabelle

He's been so very brave and it's impossible to tell

He's been so very poorly but he now looks so well

He has lost the sight in one of his lovely eyes

But battles on through his lows and his highs

He still cracks a joke or two some good but still learning

But he always tries his best with some they are recurring

A practical joker we're sure that he will become

But his efforts are still to be praised so a big well done

PANCAKE DAY

The batter's prepared and it's ready to cook

Watch out don't burn the pancakes, go and look

Tossing a pancake quite high up in the air

Hope you catch it safely but not in your hair

Once they are cooked, plated up and finally ready

Roll them up, add maple syrup then keep steady

Enjoy your pancakes, I'm sure they're tasty

Don't eat them too fast or be too quick or hasty

There are of course other toppings as an alternative

Try savoury pancakes and don't be too conservative

Served with tasty vegetables or meat with a sauce

They can in addition be enjoyed as a main course

Served up with whatever vegetables as a preference

They're healthier for you as a general reference

Whether savoury or sweet pancakes you eat today

Be sure to enjoy them as it's your pancake day

POSITIVE THINKING

Never say never is quite a strange saying

It should perhaps be we're trying to sustain

Victims of cancer should have more chances

It'll be good to have more treatment advances

To help our children and youngsters alike

To make life improvements to the max despite

Family and friends need to be more aware

To think of cancer patients and be kind and fair

The more who donate towards children with cancers

To encourage and help to find the right answers

POOR OLD FEET

I cannot get over these poor old feet

Getting sweaty and not smelling so sweet

Bathing and drying helps a little bit

Don't run regularly or it will irritate it

Feet work hard and we frequently stand

At other times we jump and then we land

Awkwardly and in the totally wrong position

Feet work very hard when they're on a mission

Such as using our feet to dance to a tune

Or prancing in the garden under the light of the moon

Our feet have a challenging job to maintain

So, try being really careful and please don't be vain

As we grow older, then so do our poor feet

Don't feel pressured to take part or compete

Sometimes our feet need plenty of rest

Don't take advantage when we're blessed

To have a pair of feet that work so very well

Rest them up sometimes so they don't
swell

RAIN

It's been raining since I woke up earlier
today

I'll need to wear a coat when I go out to
play

My bag was packed ready for school
last night

I just need my lunchbox or I will have a
fright

It looks like we'll be eating our lunch inside

It's one of those things that cannot be denied

With the rain pouring down so heavily now

Don't think there'll be much choice somehow

When I was picked up from school much later on

I accidentally stepped into a large puddle upon

Which my shoes and tights got soaked right through

But there isn't much that I can now think or do

Apart from changing out of them once I get home

I'll be happy now that I'm near to the end of the poem

RUDE SOUNDS

Sometimes we can't help making a rude noise

Just remember to stand with a certain poise

Have manners, say pardon me and say
sorry

Try not to be too nervous, please don't
worry

Watch out now your face has gone
bright red

Guess it's one of those moments we all
dread

Perhaps it was the beans or maybe the
fruit

Whatever it was it caused you to have a
loud toot

Maybe a little bit of indigestion was the
cause

Never mind it's all over and the noise
it's paused

SAUSAGE ROLL

The sausage roll can be a savoury snack

Perhaps I'm going down the wrong track

If a vegetarian option is much preferred

Just change the filling and don't be deterred

We all like something instead of a sarnie

Another filling could be chilli con carne

There's a lot to be done with a pastry square

Put savoury or sweet inside of it there

Then cut the pastry into small logs and seal

Make sure to finish them so they will appeal

An interesting roll using many different fillings

Try all sorts, that is if you're totally willing

If you're prepared to change and then adapt

You will find something that could be apt

Once ready then place on a big baking tray

In a hot oven, cook and then you're away

SEASIDE

Getting up early a stone's throw away from me

Breathing in the salty air you smell near the sea

Walking along with camera as the sun begins arising

What a beautiful sight it is but that's not surprising

A dog walker throws a stick to their little spaniel dog

He needs to be quite careful as here's the dense fog

We nod to each other as he passes by near home

He's set out much earlier so he's already had his roam

Later perhaps, he commented as he waved goodbye

I haven't got a dog I thought but as I went to notify

The stranger disappeared out of view
so I let out a sigh

Never mind I thought as I looked up at
the grey sky

Just at that moment a seagull passed on
through

I'm sure you must have guessed as
splat, a seagull poo

I felt it land in a heavy wet heap right
on my head

I wasn't happy as it's a moment anyone
would dread

SIBLINGS

Siblings are all so completely unique

They can be nice but they also retreat

Sometimes they can be sly, retreat then hit

Pinch, be nasty and then pretend to sit

Try being good, protective and give a cuddle

Rather than get yourselves into a lot of trouble

It's so much better to be very good friends

Than to drive each other around the bend

Parents cannot always be watching you know

It doesn't mean you take advantage though

You can be nice and generally both share

Instead of giving each other a horrible glare

Try to be kind and share with each other

After all you are both a sister and brother

SKYLIGHT

It's all about a night-time observation

Looking upwards at the star's constellation

Watching out in the middle of the night

The stars are all twinkling and sparkling bright

Laid out in a pattern in the dark night sky

Watching them above me with my little eye

As it becomes lighter and the darkness fades

The sky marbles into different grey shades

If cloudy then the sky could be very grey

Oh no it looks like rain so another wet day

SMELLS

There isn't very much to say about bad smells

If you move it will travel and then you can tell

Many people blame wind on their very own pet

As they are concerned someone will be direct

But a sense of detective work tells us straight

That there's no use moving so sit, stay and wait

The rude amongst us will admit to a loud guff

But the politest will say they have just had a fluff

Eventually the smell will disperse in the stale air

Then you can move without having a worry or a care

Remember dissipation can be a source of irritation

You can't control it now so you will stink out the nation

SNOWY WINTER

Grey skies approaching so we could get some snow today

We hope that the winter will be snow bombing our way

It's cold and the snow flurries have started to show

We need hats gloves and scarves to stay warm and glow

Putting your boots on your feet makes the snow seem inviting

We're also looking forward to some brilliant snowball fighting

Building a snowman takes some skill and also shaping

A carrot nose and currant eyes, with a scarf tied for draping

Must find the right hat or he just won't look the same

This could be your chance to make your claim to fame

Now you've finished playing and the snow is glistening

When you get that shout for tea, make sure you're listening

Family is watching the snow fluttering quickly to the ground

Make the most of this spell before the melting comes around

SPIDER IN MY SHOE

A spider has just crawled inside of my
left shoe

I looked down and saw it then said, 'no,
not you'

I didn't see it sneak inside the shoe you
see

As I'd popped out in the garden having
had a wee

I really don't like spiders they give me the creeps

I have dreams about them when I drop off asleep

It may sound daft but it's made me stop and think

Is it close to my water glass when I have a drink?

I really dislike spiders as sometimes they are hairy

I'm always careful now and tend to be quite wary

When I have my bath, I feel so relaxed at night

But if a spider comes close by, then I get a fright

Clear off spider, I don't want you near, you see

You look horrible and you're really scaring me

Dad came running he's heard my piercing scream

Everything is fine now so perhaps it was a dream

Watching out for spiders has become an obsession

The thought of one close or near to a possession

Spiders they're creepy as you'll find and see

Their long dangly legs and eyes that are ogling me

I'm a child who dislikes spiders hanging around

Checking high on the ceilings and also on the ground

Since finding that ugly spider inside of my shoe

I always check carefully before putting it on me too

I know it's unlikely but it doesn't stop me looking

Don't hide in my shoe spider or I'll lose my footing.

When I'm an adult they won't scare me anymore.

I'll be brave like my daddy but see them as a chore.

By the time I've grown up I'm sure I won't mind

As spiders won't be scary just something I could find

SPIDERS

Spiders vary in their size and their state

Some are small and live by my garden gate

They can spin a web in a tiny little corner

Somewhere near to where you launder

A web hangs cleverly from around a ceiling

Suddenly a spider spins down with feeling

Please be kind don't completely flatten me

I cannot scream and I'm off to have my tea

I won't come near you I'm just passing through

On the way to hiding behind your downstairs loo

Don't raise your slipper or I'll run with some pace

You cannot catch me I shall certainly win this race

STRAIGHT FROM THE HEART

This poem comes from the depths of our hearts

When our families' lives were completely ripped apart

Time spent separated was forced by his cancer care

When our grandson, Louis Knight, lost all his lovely hair

Like many other patients he had some horrible meds

That made him feel poorly and tired then confined to his bed

Unable to be visited because of the risk of contracting bugs

All anyone can do then too is send him loads of hugs

His treatment lasted for six lengthy months

Like any little boy he's pulled some funny stunts

But this brave little boy like so many others

Had treatment time just with their father or mother

It's heart wrenching to hear the full details that appear

The treatment and the care can cause infection and fear

It really brings the tears to your eyes to see a child

So helpless and in pain sometimes turn so wild

It's high dose steroids that caused the reaction

Then made Louis have a huge bad distraction

SULKY

Don't pull that face I've seen it all
before

You were sulking as you came out of
your door

I can't think what your problem is likely
to be

It can't be all bad as you will learn and
see

Learn to talk please when you have any
issues

Now please blow your nose into some tissues

Turn your mouth upwards, let's see a nice smile

Know you'll change your mind in a short while

It's such a pity that you prefer to be so sulky

You really are quite a nice girl but also quite lucky

SWIMMING

Arriving at the local swimming pool

The man at the desk is playing the fool

We asked for the temperature of the water

He didn't know although he really ought to

I've paid for my ticket to go for that swim

It's good exercise to do, to try to stay trim

Jumping in can be fun but this is disallowed

Especially when there is quite a large crowd

I think I'll try to do a few lengths in overarm

There's a swimmer ahead so I must stay calm

I'll go around them by taking a good wide berth

Swimming at some speed for all that it's worth

Next, I'll do a few lengths also in breaststroke

Then I'll take a well-earned rest as I could choke

Time to exit the pool and start drying off now

Then get showered, changed and leave somehow

It's almost time to be having a healthy lunch

So, I'll head back home to have my munch

THINKING CAP

I'm twiddling my thumbs trying to think

The teacher suggested try not to blink

Concentrate and put on your thinking cap

Don't be sidetracked by thinking claptrap

In your thoughts on the subject while in the class

Ideas they suddenly appear as clear as glass

Knowing you'll come up with many other ideas

Teacher didn't mean to pressurise then cause tears

Just a few thoughts or contributions were required

To have the rest of the class join in and be inspired

TIME ALONE

Sometimes we need our private space

To stop and think and reduce our pace

To pause for thought and take a break

Give us some space for goodness sake

We all need time just to stop and think

As other things keep us too busy to blink

Sometimes we need to empty our head

Of our thoughts before we go off to bed

 We can then relax and think straight again

The wonderful memories are still retained

TOUCAN

The toucan is a visually colourful bird

They're vocal and really like to be heard

A sleek black body with such short wings

They're wonderful and such beautiful things.

Their bright beak is lightweight and it stores food

It makes a raspberry noise that sounds quite rude

If you see it, gasp at its amazing colour wonder

Being in a forest it starts to rain and thunder

It doesn't fly too much but likes a very high tree

Where it's so much closer can socialise and see

Living in rainforests with predators like snakes

Being near the ground would be a huge mistake

TOYS

Children love playing with their toys

Whether quiet or even making a noise

Reading books or perhaps playing sport

Imaginary play with a friend's toy fort

Using remote control on a light up car

Computer games tend to be a step too far

Some are quite good but some really bad

We know that you'll have fun as you're a dad

UNWELL

When someone is poorly or not feeling well

They may not want to say or even want to tell

You cannot always see how someone is feeling

Make allowances as they could be concealing

Sticking a plaster onto a cut does not cover

What is on the inside that talking may discover

Remember to be kind to people and think first

Better fetch a drink as they could have a thirst

No point in wondering how they are feeling

When all that's needed is a chat that's revealing

WATER

Water is needed for all of us every day

We take it for granted in every way.

From washing, bathing and showering too

And when you use the toilet known as the loo

Whether a spotting shower or heavier rain

Or a pitter patter on the window pane

From snow and ice that turn into slush

Or a water leak that turns into a gush

A swim in the sea or a swimming pool

Drinking water that is clean and cool

Heating a house when weather is cold

To removing some horrible nasty mould

Putting the kettle on to boil for a hot tea

To turning on the hose and watering a tree

How lucky we are to have a water supply

When other countries have already run dry

It doesn't seem right that all aren't equal

Putting us at risk with water that's lethal

Surely there's more that can be done for them

To allow water supplies to be equal then

Appreciating some of us are doing all of this

But not enough is being done so it's hit and miss

If my health allowed me to travel around

Then I 'd do something to help with under the ground

How lucky we are to have water flowing freely

When others can't drink it when needed essentially

WIDE AWAKE GRANDAD

Grandad is sitting in his comfy armchair

Occasionally standing for a little fresh air

He observes everything that is going on

As he sings along to a nineteen sixties song

He has a few issues with hearing and his ears.

He thought he heard someone who said cheers

Tapping his foot loudly to a tune he remembers

He puts his Christmas hat on as it is December

The grandchildren smile as he ties up his laces

Grandad sings out of tune and so he disgraces

You should see the beaming smile on their little faces

Grandad's happy to hear them all reading so well

Don't be too deceived as only lots of time will tell

WOOD PIGEON

There's a pigeon in the garden with very few brains

He likes eating and preening especially when it rains

He wobbles and pecks as he moves slowly along

Watching other birds is like him playing ping pong

Once he gets bored, he flies high upon our roof

He can be seen dropping pigeon poo and is all aloof

Beware if you poke your head right out of the house

Or a dropping could land and you could have a douse

If you see a pigeon, be sure to look up in the sky

As it could be your head next time as he flies by

<u>ZOO</u>

Let's go and visit Chessington Zoo today

There'll be plenty to see, let's get on our way

The monkeys will usually be so entertaining

Hoping it's sunny and it won't start raining

We will be taking a plentiful picnic with us

There'll be lots to eat without too much fuss

Salads and sandwiches and savoury things

Such as spareribs and some chicken wings

Plenty of fun to entertain all of you

We know you'll enjoy it just as much as we do

THE AUTHOR

Linda Knight lives in Hampshire,
England and during the enforced covid

lockdowns discovered her ability to write and since then, has penned two novels, a short story, her first poetry book and an autobiography detailing the abuse suffered during her childhood at the hands of those who should have protected her.

This, her second collection of published poetry, is dedicated to the bravery of her youngest Grandson thankfully in remission from his battle with a childhood cancer with the intention that 100% of the proceeds from the book sales will be donated to Young Lives v. Cancer, a charity that provides much needed support to young sufferers and their families.

Linda enjoys her writing and it is this creative talent that keeps her going in times of adversity caused by being clinically extremely vulnerable as a result of rheumatology and respiratory conditions and the immune suppressive medications that have become a daily necessity.

She is happily married to Tony who has been her soulmate for over 46 years.

THANK YOU

Thank you for purchasing my book and donating towards :

https://www.younglivesvscancer.org.uk/life-with-cancer/

100% of the sales proceeds will be donated to the charity.

Any further donations to the above charity would be greatly appreciated.

Kindly donate to enable all families who have been or are going through cancer with children or young adults so they may get the help and support that they need from those who can help.

Printed in Great Britain
by Amazon